Volume One

Adventures of the Monkey King

Written by Lynn Xie, Rachel Albright

Illustrated by Jiaxuan Ma, Lynn Xie

Edited by Bruce Albright, Arielle Isack

ACKNOWLEDGMENTS

By Lynn Xie

==================<<>>====================

First, special thanks to my dearest daughter *Nina*. She inspired me to write the series *Wukong*. The stories of the Monkey King not only brought back many fond memories of my happy childhood, but they also contained so much positive energy of adventure, bravery, persistence and loyalty. My darling daughter has always been that happy, beautiful, kind and smart girl in my heart.

I am forever indebted to my beloved Mom. Her generosity, compassion and tenacity are the priceless legacy that she gave me. She will be forever remembered as an outstanding scientist and a model mother in my mind.

I want to express my deepest appreciation to my dear friend and co-writer, *Racheal Albright*. With her help and support, *Wukong* ebook and paperback have been published at Amazon.com. Her great passion, keen insight, and down to earth spirit bring this well-known classic story to the children around the world.

Special thanks go to our talented artist *Jiaxuan Ma* who designed more than 30 colored illustrations for the series *Wukong*. His creative artwork vividly depicts various characters in the book. Recently he found his true love and got married. I wish him and his wife good luck and great happiness.

A million thanks to our English editor *Bruce Albright and Arielle Isack* who did meticulous editing. Their valuable advices made the series *Wukong* possible. Thrie great contribution is truly appreciated and admired.

Finally, on this New Year's Day, I hope the story of *Wukong* can bring excitement and happiness to children all over the world.

January 1st, 2021   California, USA

 1. Stone Monkey

Long ago and far away, there stood an enchanted mountain rising above the waves of a vast ocean. Flowers and fruits covered every peak, slope and valley of the mountain, and many animals roamed the dense jungle in search of food or fun. On the highest point of the mountain, there was a huge boulder, so perfectly round and scarily slippery that no beasts or birds dared to touch it. Many seasons came and went, the boulder remained, getting shinier and brighter with each downpour of the rain and every kiss of the Sun. The boulder was visible from every place on the mountain. It was so huge and so constant that all creatures in the jungle learned to use the boulder as a compass when hunting.

One stormy night, deafening thunder roared in the dark and blinding lightning struck the mountain over and over. Shaken and scared by the sound and fury of the storm, all the animals hid under the dense jungle foliage and watched the lightning strike the mysterious boulder. Suddenly, they heard an ear-splitting explosion from the top of the mountain. The sound of the blast echoed in the valley for a long time, like nothing the animals had ever heard before. Only when the rosy fingers of dawn began to touch the top of the jungle did the storm finally stop

That morning, a group of monkeys emerged from the forest, jabbering about last night's violent storm and the loud noise they heard.

"What do you think happened last night, Grandpa White Eyebrows?" A young monkey asked an old monkey. If anyone knew, it was Grandpa White Eyebrows, the wisest creature in the jungle.

"Well, my child, I guess..." White Eyebrows stopped in the middle of the sentence, looking first bewildered, then terrified.

All the other monkeys became quiet and motionless. Had Grandpa White Eyebrows been alerted to some hidden dangers? They waited anxiously for his advice on what to do next.

As he stared into distance, the old monkey sighed deeply and pointed his finger at the top of the mountain. "Look, it's gone! The boulder is gone!"

Stunned, the other monkeys looked up and could not see the shining round rock that had just been there the night prior.

"How are we supposed to know where we are when the boulder is gone?" One monkey sighed. The others agreed. They were so distressed and worried by the disappearance of the boulder that they did not even have any appetite for morning flowers and fruits.

"Let us go up there and take a look. Maybe the boulder just fell off its place, and we can put it back," White Eyebrows suggested.

"Great idea!" "Let's go!" "Hurry up!" The monkeys rushed through the jungle and up the hill toward where the boulder once was.

It took them hours of jumping and climbing to reach the top of the mountain. They were shocked and devastated by what they saw..

The boulder was not intact, as White Eyebrows had imagined. It had shattered into a million pieces. The top of the mountain was covered in so many fragments of stone that the monkeys could hardly move around

"I guess the lighting struck the boulder and split it into pieces. There is nothing we can do now. Too bad." White Eyebrows sighed, motioning his followers to go back down the mountain before sunset.

"What is that?" One female monkey cried out loud, pointing to a small brown creature struggling to stand up in the rubble.

Blocking the sun rays from eyes with his palm, White Eyebrows took a good look at the creature. "Is that a baby monkey?!"

Despite the fragmented stone pieces covering the ground, the monkeys all rushed toward the baby in the broken rocks. What they saw in the center of the rubble was a beautiful monkey baby, staring up at them with a sweet face, gentle eyes, and a very long tail.

Curious about the baby monkey's origin, every monkey in the group talked at once, creating nothing but noise and confusion. Despite being surrounded by strangers, the baby monkey was not frightened and just looked at them curiously while sucking his big thumb.

"Quiet! Quiet!" White Eyebrows finally silenced the group and questioned the baby monkey.

"What is your name?"

The baby monkey smiled but did not answer.

"Who are your parents?"

The baby monkey smiled again and had no answer.

White Eyebrows shook his head and asked again. "Where are you from?"

The baby monkey shook his head.

"Do you know your tribe?"

Once again, the baby monkey shook his head. White Eyebrows began to frown.

While the questioning was going nowhere, one blue faced monkey could not help but laugh at the baby monkey. "You have no names and no parents. You just appeared right after the boulder was split. Maybe you were born out of the stone! You should be called Stone Monkey!"

"Right! A baby monkey was born out of a rock!" "A stone monkey?!" "What a miracle!" The monkeys nodded and hooted as they laughed at this ridiculous possibility.

The baby monkey suddenly stopped sucking his thumb and firmly nodded. "Stone Monkey! Stone Monkey!" He excitedly exclaimed.

2. Monkey See, Monkey Do

After Stone Monkey joined the tribe led by White Eyebrows, he soon learnt how to find food in the forest, swim in the river, hang upside down by his tail from trees, and all other fun ways of monkeying around in the jungle. Since he had neither parents nor siblings to look after him, he was very independent, wild, and adventurous.

He was always the first one to dash into the jungle, jump into a pond, or leap into a fight. Because of his mysterious origin and bold behavior, other mother monkeys did not feel comfortable having their babies hanging around him. But Stone Monkey had no problems with other monkeys shunning him. He was just happy to have a family. Besides, White Eyebrows was fond of him from the beginning, always ready to teach him knowledge about the jungle, the mountain and the ocean, all the wisdom which other monkeys were not interested in.

One mid-summer night, underneath a full moon shining bright and beautiful over the jungle, Stone Monkey and White Eyebrows were taking a stroll after dinner, while other monkeys were playing near a lily pond. Suddenly Blueface cried out, "Oh, no, the Moon has fallen into the pond!"

The other monkeys heard the cry and ran towards the pond. There it was, the silvery, gigantic Moon floating helplessly on the mirror-like surface of the pond. "We have to do something!" One monkey said.

"Let us fish it out and keep it for ourselves." said another one with a giggle.

But how to fish the Moon out of the water? Blueface jumped onto a branch leaning over the pond and hooked himself upside down onto the tree with his hind legs and tail. Another monkey got the same idea and leaped into Blueface's arms, letting him hold his feet. One by one, the monkeys joined together to form a chain. Only Mimi, the youngest baby, was left in the trees.

The monkey at the end of the chain gently touched the moon in the water, which was immediately broken into shiny pieces and dissolved into ripples.

"Where did the Moon go?" the bewildered monkeys asked.

"It went back up to the sky. What you saw in the water was only a reflection. Isn't it fun to hang upside down from the tree?" Stone Monkey teased them from ashore.

All the monkeys looked up as he spoke. Yes, as Stone Monkey said, the Moon was shining in the sky, bright and beautiful. Relieved, they all jumped into the pond and happily splashed water.

Mimi's mother did not want to leave her baby alone for too long, so she was the first to come out of the water and look around for her baby. To her surprise and horror, she could not find Mimi anywhere.

"Help! Help!" She cried, "Mimi is missing."

White Eyebrows immediately jumped on to the branch and ordered all the monkeys to search for Mimi. Soon they heard a faint cry of Mimi from a deep hole in the tree. The hole was very deep, and Mimi was too young and weak to climb out by herself. The monkeys discussed for a long time but could not reach an agreement on how to rescue the baby.

While others were busy talking, Stone Monkey cut some vines from a tree and carefully dropped the vine into the tree hole. Mimi grabbed onto the lifeline that Stone Monkey gave her and, while everyone else was squabbling, was successfully rescued out of the tree hole.

From that night on, the monkey tribe began to appreciate Stone Monkey as a valuable member of their group. Monkey moms gradually felt comfortable letting him play with their kids, and White Eyebrows continued mentoring him about the ways of the world.

3. Water Curtain Cave

One blazing hot afternoon, to escape the exhausting heat, the tribe of White Eyebrows found a cool spot in the water of a shallow creek. They played in the water for a while, but quickly got bored. One monkey suggested they go upstream to see the origin of the creek. The monkeys all agreed, and Stone Monkey dashed to the front of the troop to lead the exploration.

When they finally reached the head of the stream, they found a huge waterfall coming down from the top of a hill. Like an enormous water curtain blowing in the wind, it sprayed tiny drops of water all over the place, dissipating heat and dust from the air. Vegetation around the waterfall was exceptionally lush. Flowers and fruit weighted down tree branches over the water. The monkeys were thrilled to have found such a beautiful place. They ate and played till they were tired. Hanging upside down from a tree, a bunch of young monkeys nudged each other and said, "Does anybody dare to go into the waterfall to see what is behind it?"

"The water is pounding down like roaring thunder. It might be too dangerous," a short-tail monkey timidly answered.

"There is nothing to look at. I am sure that it is just another giant piece of rock," Blueface said with confidence.

Stone Monkey disagreed, saying "it might be something really interesting. We should go and take a look."

Before they ventured to the waterfall, White Eyebrows, who had been sitting on a tree branch, cleared his throat and said: "My children, I have served as the leader of our tribe for many seasons now. I am getting older and weaker by the day, and I would like to choose the next leader for our family."

All the young monkeys became quiet, waiting patiently for White Eyebrows to announce who the next leader would be. Looking at their eager faces, White Eyebrows continued: "The next leader has to be someone wise and brave. Most importantly, it has to be someone willing to help and defend all the family members. Today we have the perfect opportunity to select the future leader of the family. Whoever has the courage to discover the secret behind the waterfall is going to be our next leader!"

Before White Eyebrows finished his speech, Stone Monkey jumped off the tree and climbed to the top of a rock overlooking the waterfall. "I will do it!" he shouted while diving into the waterfall.

The entire monkey tribe held their breath as they saw the tiny body of Stone Monkey disappear into the crushing water. It seemed unlikely that anyone, especially a monkey so small, could survive so much force. Would they ever see him again? They all wondered.

While the tribe waited to see if he survived, Stone Monkey emerged behind the waterfall and saw that there was a huge cave behind it. He came out of the water and went inside. What a magical place it was! The cave was big, bright and sparkling inside. It had stones of all shapes and sizes. Some looked like tables and chairs, some like beds and benches, and some even like bowls and plates.

Overjoyed, Stone Monkey rushed out of the cave and jumped out of the waterfall. The monkey tribe cheered when they saw his head emerging from the water.

"Come, come with me!" Stone Monkey said, wiping water away from his face.

"What did you see?" White Eyebrows asked.

"A home! I found us a home!" Stone Monkey finally caught his breath, and urged others to come with him, "Behind the waterfall is a cave, spacious and beautiful. It even has stone furniture in it."

"What?!" "Unbelievable!" "Impossible!" Lots of monkeys were skeptical. But White Eyebrows trusted Stone Monkey. He followed Stone Monkey to dive into the waterfall. One by one, other monkeys went through the waterfall to go inside the cave. A few mother monkeys did not want to scare their babies by going through the torrents. They anxiously waited outside and did not know what to do. Stone Monkey led a group of young monkeys to gather some banana palm leaves to cover the faces of the baby monkeys. Finally, the last group of mothers and babies made their way into the cave.

It was a crazy playground inside of the cave. Monkeys were busy moving stone furniture around and playing on them. After many hours of chasing, laughing and jumping, the monkeys finally quieted down, and White Eyebrows brought Stone Monkey in front of the crowd.

"My children! How lucky we are to have such a wonderful cave to be our home. We now have a roof over our heads, beds to sleep in and even a waterfall as a curtain. We will never be bothered by bad weather now, and we must thank Stone Monkey who found us such a great home!" All of them agreed and gave Stone Monkey a roaring cheer.

"As I promised, whoever dared to explore behind the waterfall should be our next leader." White Eyebrows pointed to Stone Monkey and said, "He has done that. Now, let us all recognize him as our new leader."

White Eyebrows was the first to rub his nose on Stone Monkey's tail. One by one, the monkeys followed White Eyebrows' example to show their love and respect.

 # 4. Defending the Home

    Stone Monkey and his tribe found a piece of paradise in the Water Curtain Cave. With abundant food and fresh water nearby, they spent their days doing nothing but playing around. One day after dinner, while some monkeys were swimming in the pond outside the water curtain cave and others were having fun in the trees, only the youngest and oldest monkeys stayed behind in the cave. Suddenly Stone Monkey and his pals heard sharp screams of "Help!" "Help!" behind the waterfall. They immediately got out of the water and rushed inside the cave.

    What they saw totally stunned them. A giant python had sneaked unnoticed inside the cave and opened its big mouth ready to swallow anything in front of it. Shocked but not scared, Stone Monkey stepped up to the python and ordered it to leave. The python did not respond, opening its gaping mouth even wider and slithered even closer to Stone Monkey. "Be careful!" other monkeys cautioned Stone Monkey. Having no fear, Stone Monkey angrily jumped on the back of the python and began to punch its head.

    The python got angry, sticking its forked tongue out and swinging its powerful tail back and forth. Stone Monkey kept pounding on the slippery body of the python but failed to scare it away. All of a sudden, Stone Monkey lost his balance and fell from the back of the python onto the ground. Before any other monkeys could reach him, the python coiled its body tightly around Stone Monkey and began to squeeze. Stone Monkey could neither move nor breathe. White Eyebrows, Blueface and others tried to rescue Stone Monkey by poking the eyes and nostrils of the python, but their efforts did not work. The python just got angrier, squeezing Stone Monkey even harder. Seeing Stone Monkey's suffering, White Eyebrows let out a battle cry and jumped right in front of the mouth of the python, grabbing its swinging forked tongue. Surprised, the python began to loosen its grip on Stone Monkey. Seizing the opportunity, Blueface pulled Stone Monkey away from the python.

As soon as he was out of danger, Stone Monkey broke off a stone table leg and rushed to help White Eyebrows, who was barely holding on to the tongue of the python. "Greedy worm, leave my grandpa alone," Stone Monkey yelled while sticking the stone table leg into the open mouth of the python.

As Stone Monkey expected, the python got very angry and tried to bite him. The crushing jaws of the python did not hurt Stone Monkey or White Eyebrows, however, because the stone table leg prevented the jaws from closing. Stone Monkey, White Eyebrows and their tribe members pushed the python, now with jaws that could not close, out of their cave and into the water.

"May the water take this beast to the East Ocean and never come back!" said White Eyebrows.

"Does the stream in front of our cave flow to the East Ocean?" Stone Monkey asked.

"Yes, Stone, I mean to tell you......." Before White Eyebrows could finish his sentence, he passed out. The venom from the python had weakened him so much that he had to sleep for seven days and seven nights to recover from it.

When White Eyebrows finally woke up, he noticed the Water Curtain Cave was so noisy, as monkeys from other tribes bustled in the cave. "What is going on?" White Eyebrows asked Stone Monkey, who now sat on a high platform in the cave directing the busy movement of new monkeys.

"After the python incident, I realized that our cave is too big for a small tribe like ours," Stone Monkey said, "Dangerous creatures like that python can sneak in without detection. We need more folks to help us guard our home." Stone Monkey pointed to some big monkeys standing next to him. "So, I went around the mountain and asked them to join us here. They are happy to share the safety of our cave and help us guard our home." The big monkeys bowed to White Eyebrows. "What a great idea!" White Eyebrows tried to applaud but realized that his paws were covered with a sticky green paste. "What is that?" he asked.

"Oh, while you were sleeping, one of our new family friends, a medicine monkey, examined your hands and put some herbs on you to extract the snake poison from you." said Stone Monkey while giving White Eyebrows a hug. "Grandpa, I am so happy that you finally woke up."

Realizing that Stone Monkey had saved his life, White Eyebrows was very moved and patted Stone Monkey with the back of his hand.

White Eyebrows totally recovered several months later. One misty morning, he and Stone Monkey walked along the creek to inspect the new barrier the monkeys had built along the riverbank.

"No snakes can ever cross those barriers. Our home is totally safe, Grandpa!" Stone Monkey proudly said.

"You did a great job indeed, Stone." said White Eyebrows. "But the next enemy may not be a python. What if it is a creature with weapons, or even magic power? What then? Will those barriers you built be able to stop them?"

Stone Monkey became speechless. He had no answer. "What should I do?" he finally asked.

"You should learn. Only a learned leader has the true ability to protect his family and friends," White Eyebrows said slowly.

5. Journey to an Unknown Land

"We will miss you!"

"Safe journey!"

"Send us greetings by the pelicans!"

"Take a few more coconuts and bananas with you..."

Standing on the riverbank, hundreds of monkeys from Water Curtain Cave waved their good-byes to Stone Monkey, who decided to embark on a journey to learn the art of war and power of magic. He did not know how he would acquire this knowledge, but after speaking to White Eyebrows, he knew he would find a knowledgeable Master somewhere someday.

The wisest monkeys got together to help Stone Monkey build a simple bamboo raft. On a breezy day, Stone Monkey sailed towards the great East Ocean, from where he started the journey to an unknown land.

    Stone Monkey was excited to set sail to the unknown land, but after a few days he became homesick. He wanted to turn the raft around and rush back to see his family and friends. But he knew that the great burden of defending his home now rested on his shoulders. He had to leave his loved ones behind in order to learn the power of magic in a faraway land.

    On the vast ocean, Stone Monkey's raft was so small that it was like a tiny leaf floating on the sea. Many passing seabirds noticed him and sometimes they flew down to chat with him. They all found him a little crazy. Who had heard of a monkey sailing across the ocean in order to learn the power of magic? They often flew away while laughing at him. However, they were also quite impressed by him, so they talked about this brave little monkey among themselves. Some birds admired his courage so much that they would fly next his raft to keep him company.

"Only the immortals have the power of magic," said an old seagull.

"Where can I find them?" asked Stone Monkey.

"My great-great-great grandfather once flew by one of the islands inhabited by those immortals. I believe it was south of where you are now, but how can you get there on such a tiny raft?"

"Well, I have to try. If I don't, I will never get there," Stone Monkey answered.

"Good luck to you then." The seagull shook his head and flew away.

One stormy night, the wind became so strong that Stone Monkey had to hold the side of the raft tightly. Gusty winds blew at him for hours, and he became so tired that he fell asleep. All of a sudden, he was awakened by the fierce shaking of the raft. The wind got stronger as the rain poured down. The raft was tossed around by the angry roaring waters, up and down like a helpless creature caught in the wind. A huge wave hit the raft, and smashed it into pieces.

Stone Monkey fell into the water and struggled desperately to catch his breath. At that moment, a giant sea turtle swam swiftly in an effort to reach Stone Monkey just before he was about to sink. The Sea turtle used all its strength to push Stone Monkey above the water with its hard shell back from underneath. The sea turtle saved Stone Monkey's life. The storm eventually quieted down when the Sun began to rise.

"Thousands of thanks for saving my life." Said Stone Monkey to the sea turtle.

"No problem. We sea turtles are born lifeguards of the ocean. Sit on my back and hold on to my neck, but not too tightly. I don't want to be choked," the turtle said and giggled, "by the way, what is a monkey doing in the middle of an ocean? I heard you guys like to live in the mountains."

"I am in search of a master to teach me magic power." Stone Monkey said.

"So, you are the crazy monkey the birds have been talking about! Wow! Crossing the ocean on your own, you are totally wild!" The sea turtle was truly impressed.

"I lost my raft in the storm. What can I do now?" Stone Monkey became worried.

"Well, I like crazy dudes who dare to pursue their dreams," the sea turtle said, "You know what, I go around the world twice a year and know every island. Just tell me where you want to go and I will take you there," the sea turtle happily offered.

"I want to find where the immortals live and learn from them." Stone Monkey said.

"The Island of Immortals. I know where it is. By the way, my name is Taotao, " Taotao was a very chatty and friendly guy, so he and Stone Monkey quickly became good friends.

It took them many months to swim across the ocean. One beautiful morning the Sun was rising slowly above the horizon, they landed on a white sandy beach. "This is your stop, dude." The sea turtle let Stone Monkey off his back.

"Thank you so much, Taotao. Do you know where I should go from here?" Stone Monkey asked.

"I don't. You have to find your own way from now on, my friend." Taotao waved goodbye to Stone Monkey as he returned to the ocean.

6. Island of Immortals

After landing on an unfamiliar shore. Stone Monkey wondered which direction he should go in. After a moment of hesitation, he decided to go east, following the direction of the sunrise. He didn't know how long he had walked until he finally heard the sound of some animals in the forest. He was very pleased and sprang into the woods. There he saw several big monkeys, who looked similar to him but without fur on their faces, walking on their hind legs and making noises with each other. Stone Monkey noticed that some furless big monkeys gave small round black pebbles to others in exchange for fruit and vegetables. "They certainly look different from me and my folks. Those poor guys have no fur, so they have colorful things on their bodies to keep them warm," he thought while walking towards them, "Maybe they will share their fruit with me." For months, he had eaten nothing but seaweed on the back of the kind sea turtle.

Stone Monkey walked toward one of them with bananas in front of him, asking, "Hi, may I have a banana, please?" The guy looked stunned, staring at Stone Monkey without a word. "Would you share a banana with me, please?" Stone Monkey asked again, patient and polite. The guy screamed and ran away. He ran so fast that a piece of colorful fabric fell off his shoulder to the ground. Stone Monkey did not understand why this hairless monkey was so scared. He picked up the soft thing on the ground and ran after the guy to return it. To his surprise, every hairless monkey nearby began to scream and run as soon as they saw him. "Do I look that scary?" Stone Monkey felt hurt, because he had never been rejected by his monkey pals before.

"Hey, dude, it is useless." Stone Monkey heard someone talking to him from a tree. He looked up and saw a small, snub nose golden monkey sitting on a branch. "Are you talking to me?" Stone Monkey asked. He was happy to find someone who seemed to understand him. "Could you tell me why those hairless monkeys are running away from me? I just want to get something to eat."

"You must be new to this place." The golden monkey shook his head and sighed. According to him, the hairless monkeys walking on their hind legs were humans. They looked similar to monkeys, but they understood neither the words nor deeds of monkeys. The colorful soft things they wrap around their bodies were called clothes, and the round small black pebbles they used to get food were called money.

"Do they have magic powers?" Stone Monkey anxiously asked.

"No, most humans are busy with making money, so they can clothe and feed themselves. They don't have time for magic."

"But I heard this is the island of immortals where I can learn the power of magic." Stone Monkey was greatly disappointed.

"Well, when humans are no longer controlled by their desires to have better food or clothes, some of them indeed learn to acquire the power of magic. The ones who can live forever are regarded as immortals."

"Where are they? Where can I find them?" Stone Monkey eagerly said.

"Master Bodhi, the great immortal, supposedly lives in a hidden valley somewhere on this island. I heard that he has a magic school for humans."

"Do you know where he lives?"

"No. Even if you find him, you don't speak human language, how can he teach you anything?"

"I will learn how to be a human first then."

For the next few months, Stone Monkey visited many markets, villages and temples, carefully observing how humans interacted with each other. After much practice, he learned to dress, speak and walk like humans. He asked every fisherman, woodcutter, farmer and peddler he ran into where Master Bodhi lived, but nobody seemed to know.

One humid afternoon, Stone Monkey sat on the aerial roots of a giant Banyan tree after another day of useless searching. Suddenly, a voice from the thick leaves of the Banyan tree boomed out "Who is hanging on my beard?" Surprised, Stone Monkey jumped to the ground and stammered, "I am looking for Master Bodhi..." but before he could finish his sentence, the giant Banyan tree had disappeared, and an old man in a green robe with a long white beard appeared in front of him. "I am Master Bodhi. Why are you looking for me?"

"I want to study magic with you!" Stone Monkey said excitedly.

"Not everyone deserves to master the power of magic. Tell me something about you so I know that you are worthy."

Stone Monkey told his life story to the master. "I promised my folks to learn the power of magic to protect them. So please teach me," he begged.

"So, you sailed thousands of miles across the ocean to learn from me. How courageous!" Master Bodhi nodded, "What is your name?"

"My folks call me Stone because I was born out of a piece of stone." "You need an official name to enter my school of magic," said Master Bodhi. "How about Sun Wukong? Sun is your surname, indicating that you come from a monkey family. Wukong means making something out of nothing." "Thank you, Master. From now on I have a name: Sun Wukong." Wukong bowed to Master Bodhi.

"Follow me, Wukong." Master Bodhi led Wukong cross over two mountains, finally they arrived at the gate of a temple. A boy opened the door.

7. School of Magic

Wukong spent the first six years at Master Bodhi's magic school learning how to read books, write calligraphy, practice martial arts, cook meals, cut wood and even clean the house. He did everything except study magic. Every time he asked Master Bodhi about it, the Master said that the time was not right.

One day when Wukong and his classmates were attending a seminar on the power of magic, he became so excited that he began to dance around the classroom. Master Bodhi got out of his seat to scold him.

"I am sorry, Master. I was just too excited about what we are talking about," Wukong said.

"Not everybody shares your excitement. It is time for you to learn how to behave in the classroom. Do not disturb your classmates anymore." Master Bodhi patted the head of Wukong three times, putting his hands behind his back before dismissing the class. Everybody thought the Master was mad at Wukong, but the monkey had a different idea.

That night Wukong waited for the clock to strike three times before he went through the back door to Master Bodhi's bedroom. Facing the wall, the Master seemed to be in sound sleep. Wukong knelt down in front of the bed and patiently waited and waited, and finally he heard the Master asking him: "What are you doing here?"

"Master, you said today that it is time for me to learn magic. You patted me three times on the head to signal the time for me to be here. You also put your hands behind your back to let me know that I should come here through the back door. Here I am, ready to learn the secrets of magic from you." The Master was very pleased to see that Wukong understood his intention perfectly. "Wukong, the mystical power you are about to learn is going to transform you from nobody to somebody."

He began to teach Wukong how to gain the mystical powers of the universe.

During his years of studying with Master Bodhi, Wukong often thought about his Grandpa White Eyebrows and his family behind the waterfall. He even tried in vain to send them messages through pelicans or cranes. Wukong worked very hard in the magic school because he figured that the sooner he graduated, the sooner he could see his home and family again.

The Master taught Wukong how to cast spells, shift forms and walk in the sky. Wukong liked to boast, even though the Master often reminded him not to show off in front of other classmates for fear that they would be jealous of him. One day after lunch a classmate asked Wukong, "Hey, dude, where do you go every night? I have noticed that you are never in your bed after midnight."

"The Master gives me special instructions at night," Wukong answered without thinking.

"What have you learned?"

"Lots of things, form shifting, sky walking, etc."

"Wow, could you show us how you walk in the sky?"

Wukong enjoyed the admiration of others so much that he forgot what the Master had told him about boasting. He stretched a bit before he jumped into the sky, grabbing a piece of passing cloud as a floating cushion. He hovered in the sky for a while and came down to receive cheers from his peers.

Loud cheers woke up the Master who was napping inside his room.

"What is going on?" Master Bodhi asked.

"Wukong is showing off his new skills," someone answered.

Master Bodhi sighed and shook his head.

When Wukong came for his midnight study that night, Master Bodhi looked very disappointed. Wukong immediately realized that he had been wrong not to follow the advice of the Master. "I am sorry, Master. I will never show off again," Wukong begged for forgiveness.

"OK, remember this lesson and I will forgive you," The Master agreed. "By the way, Wukong, the sky walking skills you showed off this afternoon were only beginner stuff. To enhance your speed, I can teach you a new technique, which is called the somersault leap."

Somersault leaps were truly powerful sky walking skills. With only one leap, Wukong could cover eighteen thousand miles. The master also perfects his form shifting skills. He could successfully transform himself into seventy-two different types of things by a magic spell.

Unlike Grandpa White Eyebrows, who always gave Wukong his undivided attention, Master Bodhi showed his affection by assigning him challenging homework and difficult tasks. Wukong understood that Master Bodhi cared deeply for him because the strict training he received quickly transformed him from a naive little monkey into an accomplished magician, as well as a Kungfu master.

Many months passed, and Wukong had a party with his classmates. After a few drinks, someone said, "Hey, Wukong, you mentioned that you can also shift forms. Could you show us something that you can change into?"

"No, I shouldn't." Wukong learnt his lesson from the last time.

"Why not? Are you afraid for us to see the imperfection in your form shifting?" another classmate challenged him.

"Certainly not. I am good at everything I do," Wukong answered with great pride, "what do you want me to shift into?"

"How about a pine tree?"

Unable to resist an opportunity to show off, Wukong instantly transformed himself into a pine tree. It was so real that a squirrel climbed on top of him and began to chew on pine cones. Wukong felt so tickled that he started to giggle.

But no one was laughing with him. Wukong looked down and saw the disappointed face of Master Bodhi. "I give each student different instructions according to their talents. Others may not be able to learn what you can do. By showing off in front of them, you only cause envy and discord. Wukong, it is time for you to go home," said the Master.

Knowing that he had disobeyed and disappointed the Master, tears welled up in Wukong's eyes. "Please, please give me another chance," he begged.

Master shook his head and let out a sigh.

"I am sorry, Master," Wukong choked up while bowing to the Master. "I shall bring you honor by using the knowledge you have taught me."

"The greatest glory a teacher can expect is to see a student fulfill his potential. Wukong, use your power and courage for the good." Master Bodhi said, patting him on his head.

8. Coming Home

The journey that used to take Stone Monkey months to complete was now only half of a somersault leap away for Wukong. Standing in front of the Water Curtain Cave, Wukong was very proud of his accomplishments. "Hi, my family, I am back!!" Wukong was waiting for cheers from his adoring tribes. Nothing but his own voice echoed in the valley. Wukong was quite surprised and a little scared. "Anybody home? Blueface… Mimi..."

Finally, a shadow emerged from the grass near the waterfall. "Who is yelling here? This is the summer home of our King Grizzly! All monkeys have to move out by midnight today," a nasty jackal barked at Wukong. "You are a monkey. Good, come down to help us clean the place."

"What are you talking about?" Wukong said. With his magic powers, he snapped his finger and made the jackal stop barking and become stiff as a frozen statue.

Wukong jumped through the waterfall and went inside the cave. It was not the beautiful fairy tale cave that he remembered from years ago. All the stone furniture was gone and the ground was covered with a layer of stinky mold. A few jackals and hyenas were running around with bones in their mouths, but there were no monkeys in sight. "Grandpa, Blueface, Mimi, I am home," he cried out, "Where are you all?"

"I am here," a weak voice came from the depths of the cave.

Following the sound, Wukong found a side cave where White Eyebrows was lying on the ground. Beside him was Blueface, by now an old monkey, too. "I am home, Grandpa," Wukong told White Eyebrows. Grabbing Wukong's hands, White Eyebrows said, "I am glad that you are finally back. Don't worry about me. Grizzly has kidnapped most of our folks and held them as hostages. He wanted to kick me out of our cave and the deadline is tonight. Find our folks and save the cave."

Blueface informed Wukong that King Grizzly was a giant bear with enormous power. He used his superior strength to enslave almost all the creatures on this mountain, and now wanted to occupy the Water Curtain Cave. Wukong assured White Eyebrows and Blueface that he had acquired not only the power of magic, but also the art of war. He would avenge the entire monkey clan tonight. "But you are so small," Blueface said with a little skepticism.

"Don't worry, Blue. Just find me a stone bowl," Wukong said with great confidence.

When King Grizzly came to the Water Curtain Cave to do the final inspection before moving in, he was surprised to see Blueface was waiting for him at the waterfall. "I heard you and that old monkey refused to leave. Have you changed your mind?" Grizzly asked.

"Your majesty, the old monkey was too silly to make sense. I have decided on my own to welcome you to the Water Curtain Cave. Please accept this bowl of homemade lemonade as my welcome gift," Blueface presented a stone bowl with yummy juice to Grizzly while adding, "It was freshly made with the sweetest honey, your majesty."

"Honey? Let me just try a bit." Grizzly took a small sip and boy, it was so tasty that he drank up the whole bowl of juice in one gulp. "Now show me around in my new home," said Grizzly while tossing the bowl back at Blueface.

"Now I think you should leave while you can," Blueface replied.

"Are you mad? I am King Grizzly the Great, the biggest and meanest bear in the whole mountain!" Grizzly began to roar, and the volley echoed his angry booming voice.

"Quit scaring my friend, you stinky beast." Grizzly heard a voice coming from his own stomach.

"What is going on?" Grizzly felt bewildered.

"Hey, you stupid monster, our chief has just returned with magical power. He transformed himself into that delicious juice you just drank. He is inside your stomach now," Blueface proudly announced.

"Yeah? If he is just some juice in my tummy, I will just pee him out!" Grizzly did not want to show how scared he was.

"No, you won't," Wukong answered inside of Grizzly, "I heard you had beaten up all the animals in this mountain, so why don't you pick on someone your own size?" Wukong began to punch Grizzly's heart and guts from inside Grizzly's enormous belly.

"Ouch! Ouch! Please stop! I will do anything you want," Grizzly could not stand the sharp pain and begged Wukong to stop.

"I have three requests: first, you return my folks and all the other animals to their homes; second, you return all the furniture you stole from our cave; third, you and your followers never come anywhere near the Water Curtain Cave from now on," Wukong said.

"Yes, yes, I will do anything. Come out, please!!!" Grizzly pleaded.

"No, I will only come out after you release all the animals you imprisoned." Wukong said firmly.

Grizzly ordered his followers to free all the animals and return the furniture they took. What a great scene of reunion! Thousands upon thousands of monkeys, boars, goats, rabbits, deer and squirrels were freed. They all rushed to find their own loved ones. Thousands of monkeys came back to the Water Curtain Cave, where White Eyebrows and Blueface were waiting to welcome them.

After the last monkey returned, Wukong transformed into a bee and came out of Grizzly's belly through his nose. Seeing that Wukong was just a tiny bee, Grizzly got very mad and tried to crush him.

Now certain that Grizzly's mean nature could never change, Wukong stung Grizzly's nose and mouth, which soon swelled up like a balloon. Humiliated and injured, Grizzly ran away with his jackal and hyena buddies and never dared to return.

9. Reunion with a Friend

After Wukong restored peace to the mountain, all the animals he saved now wanted him to be their king. They got together in front of the Water Curtain Cave and chanted:

"What do we want?"

"A monkey king!"

"When do we want it?"

"Now!"

Feeling loved and respected, Wukong happily came in front of the crowd with White Eyebrows at his side. "What do I do, Grandpa?" Wukong asked.

"Do as you wish!" White Eyebrows exclaimed.

"My family, my friends, I hear you! I will accept your wish to be your king. I will lead you as fairly as I can and protect our mountains as much as my ability allows me," Wukong announced to the animals.

Like a good king, he walked among the crowds to shake their paws and kiss their babies. But he soon noticed that almost every monkey, rabbit, deer or goat he contacted covered their noses when shaking paws with him. Worst of all, every baby he touched cried out of control. "What is going on, Grandpa? I thought they liked me."

Feeling embarrassed, Wukong secretly asked White Eyebrows, who now had to walk with a crutch.

"My dear child and my great king, you just came out of the fat belly of a bear. To be honest with you, you stink!" White Eyebrows whispered.

Wukong smelled his armpits and said, "I do need a bath. Tell others to party on. I will be back soon."

Wukong did not want to bathe in front of the Water Curtain Cave while thousands of animals were celebrating. He rushed to a beach open to the great East Ocean and took a nice long bath. After washing off the slime, Wukong comfortably sunbathed on a rock, half asleep. "Hey, Stone, is that you?" Wukong heard a familiar voice from somewhere...

Wukong slowly opened his eyes and saw a big smiling face of a sea turtle. "Taotao! Fancy meeting you here. How are you?" Wukong gave the turtle a big hug. "What brings you here?" he asked.

"Well, I got tired of being a traveling turtle, so I settled down and found a job in the palace of the Dragon King of the East Ocean. What has happened to you since we parted our ways?" Taotao was curious.

Wukong told Taotao all about his study with Master Bodhi and how he became the King of his mountain home. "Come to visit the

Water Curtain Cave with me. I want to introduce you to my family," Wukong invited Taotao.

"Well, I'd love to, but I am on an official mission," Taotao sighed. "The Dragon King of the East Ocean has a son who is crazy about playing chess, which has caused many problems in the underwater world."

"I love to play chess, too. What is wrong with that?" Wukong was confused.

"Well, chess is a fun game if players play on chess boards with chess pieces. But our Prince likes to use real sea creatures to play chess. For every game, our Prince selects 32 sea creatures, 16 on each side. It always ends with a slaughter of dozens of shrimps, crabs and lobsters. Our King is very concerned with his son's hobby and tries to stop him. But the Prince said that he would only quit if someone could defeat him. I am on my way to find the best chess player in the world to stop the Prince."

"I am the best chess player in my magic class. Would you take me to play with him?" Wukong felt the need to stop this Prince.

Taotao thought for a while and said, "I have traveled the world in the past few months but failed to find a player to beat the Prince. Why not give you the chance? Come with me, my friend!"

Taotao and Wukong dove into the ocean and swam to the Crystal Palace where the Dragon King of the East Ocean lived. At the gate Wukong was stopped by shrimp captains who were standing guard. Taotao introduced Wukong as their Dragon King's honorable guest. The shrimp let them in.

Taotao announced Monkey King's arrival. Dragon King of the East Ocean greeted Wukong, but he was not impressed by the insignificant size and look of the monkey. "You mean you want to play chess with my son, who is the best chess player of the water world?" The Dragon King smugly looked up and down at Wukong. "You look nothing but a skinny little monkey to me."

Wukong ignored the insults and said, "I am not any ordinary monkey! I am the Monkey King with magic power. I am the defender of all mountain creatures. We are actually neighbors. Let me introduce myself. My name is Sun Wukong, and I just graduated from a magic school. I was the best chess player in my class. I'd like to play chess with your son and teach him a lesson."

"Are you sure that you are a king?" The Dragon King of the East Ocean laughed. "Even my lowest ranking palace guards dress better than you are. You don't even have armor or a single weapon, so how dare you to call yourself the defender of all mountain creatures?" Compared to the Dragon King's splendid robes, what Wukong was wearing was no better than rags.

"I admit that my clothes are kind of shabby and I don't have a weapon." Wukong laughed and suggested, "Do you want to make a bet? If I beat your son, you will give me some warrior clothes and a weapon of my choice."

"What if you lose?" asked the Dragon King.

"If I lose, I will never bother you again." Wukong replied.

"Done deal!" The Dragon King asked Taotao the Turtle to take Wukong to where the Prince played chess.

10. Underwater Chess Battle

In the middle of a dense kelp forest, a square of white sand was cleared out and lined with black pebbles to mark the border. Rows of shrimps, crabs, lobsters, shellfish and even turtles were lined up as chess pieces. They were in their full armor and ready for battle. The Prince of the East Ocean was a young dragon who hadn't grown wings yet. Armed with the lance of a unicorn and mounted on a giant sea horse, he was wearing a set of gold armor covered in pearls. Thousands of luminescent jellyfish lit the game while gently drifting around.

"Hey monkey, this is not one of the sissy chess games you play on land. In the water, we fight real battles. You direct your pawns and pieces and I direct mine to do real battles. We will fight to the last shrimp or crab until one side wins. Get the point?"

Even under the shifting lights of the jellyfish, Wukong could see the terrified look of the shrimps and crabs who were forced to fight to the death. He had heard from Taotao that thousands of sea creatures had already lost their lives because of the Prince's cruelty. "A good leader was someone to protect the weak," he remembered what Master Bodhi had taught him. Wukong felt very strongly that it was his duty to save the lives of the innocent sea creatures.

He smiled at the Prince and said, "thank you for explaining the rules to me, your Royal Highness. May I have a minute with my pawns and knights to discuss our battle plans?"

"It is useless, but I will let you do it. It will only prolong your misery," The Prince arrogantly agreed. Wukong gathered all his shrimp and crab soldiers together and told them his plan. Then the battle began.

The Prince ordered his pawns to immediately attack their opponents. Instead of fighting head to head, Wukong's pawns ran into the kelp forest. The Prince pawns was stunned. They did not know what to do so they stopped fighting. The Prince got mad. He jumped off his Seahorse to force his pieces to go into the kelp forest in search of their opponents. But as soon as the Prince touched the sand, one of Wukong's pawns, a shell fish who was hiding in the sand, caught his legs. Other pawns jumped on him and tied him up with the sticky kelp.

"It is time for you to surrender, little guy." Wukong exclaimed.

"You tricked me! What you did is not a chess move!" The Prince screamed at Wukong.

"Killing is not a part of a chess game either, but you have been doing that for a long time. Now you must stop!" Wukong said firmly.

"I am the only son of the Might Dragon King of the vast East Ocean. My father owns all the creatures in the water. I can do whatever I want!" The Prince yelled and transformed himself into a snake-like creature, escaping from the kelp.

With lightning speed Wukong grabbed the Prince by his neck and dragged him to see his father.

"Well, your majesty, I won." Wukong told the Dragon King while showing him his son in its serpent form.

"Oh, Mighty Monkey King, please release my son. He is just a spoiled kid. He did not mean to harm anybody." The Dragon King begged.

"I remember we had a bet. What should I ask for in return for winning?" Wukong pretended that he was thinking hard. The Dragon King immediately ordered Lieutenant Lobster and his team to bring out a selection of royal weapons from the Underwater War Chest. But Monkey King found everything they showed him boring and unimpressive.

"Captain turtle, bring that 3600-pound lance to the Monkey King!" The Dragon King ordered.

Wukong tried out the lance and complained, "Not heavy enough!"

"Major Carp, present the 7200 pounds three-pronged fork."

The Monkey King practiced a few moves with the fork and shrugged. "Still not heavy enough."

The Dragon King of the East Ocean sighed, pleading to Wukong, "The fork is the heaviest weapon in my collection. Could you release my son first and then we will hunt for a suitable weapon for you?"

"I heard that nobody is richer than the Dragon King of the East Ocean. I am sure if you look carefully in your collection, you will find something for me." Wukong said.

"Your majesty, behind our magnificent Crystal Palace there is a piece of divine iron rod which weighs 13500 pounds. If nothing satisfies the Monkey King in our arms collection, you can ask him to see if he would like to take it," The mother of the Prince whispered in the ears of the Dragon King.

"But that rod is what stabilizes the ocean floor. If we give it to him, what will happen to the ocean?" The Dragon King worried.

"We do whatever we must do to get our son back and get rid of that trouble making monkey!" the mother of the Prince angrily said.

Wukong was playing with the snake-like body of the Prince as if it was a rubber toy, squeezing it into all kinds of funny shapes. Shrimps and crabs who used to be terrified by the Prince were giggling behind their claws, sending out bubbles all over the Crystal Palace.

"Ok, Mighty Monkey King, please follow me to see the true wonder of my palace." The Dragon King led Wukong to an abyss, where a great iron rod capped with gold radiated neon-like lights. It was such a magnificent sight that Wukong couldn't help but walk up to it, marveling at its beauty and size. He noticed that there was an inscription on the rod: "This Magic Gold Clapped Iron Rod, weighing 13500 pounds, will follow your wishes."

"Can it really follow my wishes?" Wukong asked. "I wish the rod could get smaller." While he was talking, the Magic Rod began to shrink. "Could it get even smaller?" It slowly shrank to the size of a needle. Wukong picked it up and made it grow big again. He eventually found the right size and began to play with it.

Suddenly the floor of the Ocean started to tremble, and the walls of Crystal Palace began to crack. "Stop it! Stop!" The Dragon King of the East Ocean told Wukong, "Beware of the power of this rod. It has the power to stabilize or disturb the ocean itself."

"Thank you, my neighbor," Wukong happily shrank the rod to the size of a needle and tucked it behind his ear.

"Could you let my son go now?" The Dragon King pleaded again.

"Well, you also agreed to give me a new set of armor. As I remember, you said that I don't look like a king." Wukong twisted the body of the Prince like a balloon animal.

Horrified at the sight of her son's helpless form, the mother of the Prince immediately ordered mermaids to bring out all the armor from their storage. But the armor they brought was either too big or small. Nothing seemed to fit Wukong. Taotao the Turtle suggested to the Dragon King, "Your Majesty, your three brothers—the dragon kings of the West, North and South Oceans-- are all fabulously wealthy. They might have something that will fit the Monkey King."

"Great idea!" said the Dragon King of the East Ocean. He immediately had Taotao play the dragon drum to summon his brothers. The sound of the dragon drum traveled through the water at lightning speed, and the three brothers of the Dragon King soon appeared at the steps of the Crystal Palace. From the beating of the drum they learned what their brother needed, so they each came with a gift.

"Here is a golden crown with pearls," said the Dragon King of the West Ocean.

"Here is gold chainmail armor with a red cape," said the Dragon King of the North Ocean.

"Here is a pair of magic boots which can walk on clouds," said the Dragon King of the South Ocean.

With the help of Taotao, Wukong put on the magnificent crown, armor and boots brought by Dragon Kings, and they fit him perfectly.

"Thank you very much," Wukong said. He smiled as he looked at himself in the coral framed mirror. When he returned the Prince to his parents, he asked them not to spoil the kid anymore. "If you dare to hurt another creature again, I will spank you with my new Magic Rod," Wukong threatened the Prince, who whimpered in fear.

Taotao and others were grateful to Wukong for saving countless sea creatures' lives. They waved good-bye to Wukong as he swam up to the surface.

Coming out of the water, Wukong heard loud cheers and noises. As it turned out, the mountain animals got worried after he did not return from his bath in the East Ocean, so they came to the shore to search for him. They were very happy and surprised to see him return in such a splendid outfit, and were even happier after they heard the story of how he got his powerful weapon and shiny armor.

The animals decided to throw a big party for Wukong to celebrate his victory. Everybody was drinking and eating merrily until dusk. At the end of the party, White Eyebrows cleared his throat and told all the animals: "I was fortunate enough to see Wukong grow up from a tiny little stone monkey into a smart, brave and courageous king. Now he is equipped with a wonderful weapon and a set of awesome armor. Nobody has ever seen anybody like him. I shall officially announce that he is our Monkey King the Magnificent! "

The End

Printed in Great Britain
by Amazon